MAGNUM *Images*

This book is to be returned on or before
the last date stamped below

André Deutsch

First published in Great Britain in 1990
by André Deutsch Limited
105-106 Great Russell Street, London WC1

All photographs and text © 1990 by Magnum Photos.
All rights reserved.
Printed in Hong Kong
Book design by Michael Rand and Ian Denning.

British Library Cataloguing in Publication Data
Ritual. — (Magnum images).
1. Photographs. Special subjects. Rituals
I. Magnum Photos II. Series
779.93064

ISBN 0-233-98606-5

Printed in Hong Kong by
Dah Hua Printing Press Co., Ltd.

Introduction

Magnum, the great photographic co-operative, was founded in 1947, although a number of its members had been taking superb photographs since the Thirties. In this book Magnum presents a dazzling selection of some of the finest images devoted to ritual in all its forms.

RITUAL, using the term in its broadest sense, ranges from the religious to the profane, from holy sacraments to popular celebrations, carnivals and pilgrimages, parades and political conventions, fair-grounds and children at play.

In these beautifully printed pages we can see Pope Paul in full papal regalia received by Pago Pago tribesmen in native dress.

Robert Kennedy, in his own tribal garments of top hat and tails, is officially received by Ivory Coast tribesmen wearing their own less sophisticated tribal dress.

Ritual means open-air confession in Poland, Holy Communion in Massachusetts, a Barmitzvah in New York, a mass in Paris, circumcision among the Masai, a Shinto marriage in Japan and a marriage to Christ at a convent in England. We see a beer festival in Bavaria, prayer on the oil fields of Saudi Arabia, Christmas in Hong Kong, a tea ceremony in Japan, a pyjama party in the American Mid-West and much, much more.

Ritual is inexhaustible, and this book is a worthy celebration of its riches.

Cover
David Seymour
Feast of San Gennaro,
Italy.

Frontispiece
Werner Bischof
Shinto marriage,
Japan.

James Natchwey
Military Academy,
Guatemala, 1987.

Raymond Depardon
Palace Moneda,
Chile, 1971.

Marc Riboud
British merchant,
Ghana, 1960.

Bruno Barbey
Adorned elephant,
Perheiza Festival,
Kandy, Ceylon.

René Burri
Traditional greeting,
Japan.

Josef Koudelka
Remembrance Day,
London.

Sebastiao Salgado
May Day Parade,
Moscow.

Henri Cartier-Bresson
*Boy Scout jamboree,
USA.*

Kryn Taconis
First Holy Communion,
Sardinia.

Leonard Freed
Barmitzvah,
New York.

Josef Koudelka
Baptism,
Portugal.

Ferdinando Scianna
Procession del Vendredi
Santo, Enna, Sicily.

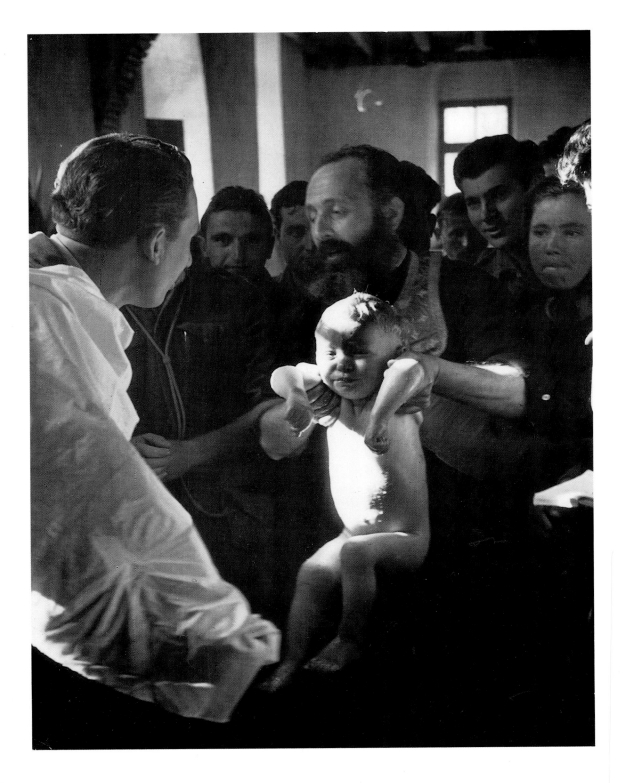

Eugene Richards
First Holy Communion,
Dorchester,
Massachusetts, USA.

Gilles Peress
Baptism, the godfather
prepares to dry
the child, Greece.

Harry Gruyaert
Festival of Cats,
Belgium.

Martine Franck
Carnival, Basle,
Switzerland.

Josef Koudelka
Carnival, Venice.

Josef Koudelka
May Day celebration,
Czechoslovakia, 1968.

Josef Koudelka
Sumara Santa Chica,
Cordoba, Spain.

Josef Koudelka
Basle Carnival,
Switzerland.

Raymond Depardon
Central Park,
New York.

Richard Kalvar
Hong Kong.

Harry Gruyaert
Stavelot Carnival,
Blancs Moussis,
Belgium.

Leonard Freed
October Beer Festival,
Bavaria, W. Germany.

Martin Parr
*Pilgrims climb to the
summit of Croagh Patrick,
Ireland.*

Josef Koudelka
*Holy Week Pilgrimage,
Cordoba, Spain.*

Bruno Barbey
*Pilgrims at Fatima,
Portugal.*

Josef Koudelka
Festa Calabrese, Italy.

Josef Koudelka
Pilgrimage to Fatima,
Portugal.

Steve McCurry
*Baptism at Christian
Rock Concert, USA.*

Josef Koudelka
*Gypsy pilgrimage reaches
Lourdes, France.*

Josef Koudelka
*Easter Passion,
Spain.*

Ferdinando Scianna
Lent Pilgrimage,
Italy.

Alex Webb
Saut D'Eau Pilgrimage,
Haiti.

Raymond Depardon
*Robert Kennedy visits
the Ivory Coast, 1961.*

Eve Arnold
*Republican Convention,
Chicago, 1952.*

Raymond Depardon
Pompidou visits Djibouti,
1973.

Costa Manos
Grief over nephew
killed in Vietnam,
South Carolina, 1966.

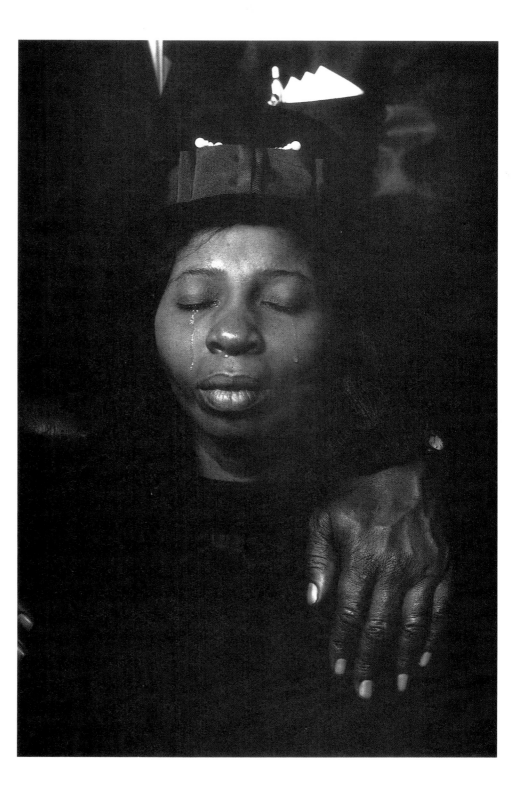

Elliott Erwitt
Funeral of John F. Kennedy,
Virginia, 1963.

Sergio Larrain
Grave,
Tierra del Fuego.

Bruno Barbey
Funeral,
Guilin, China.

Josef Koudelka
Funeral,
Czechoslovakia, 1965.

Gilles Peress
Funeral of Paul Withers,
shot by a plastic bullet,
N. Ireland, 1981.

Leonard Freed
Graveyard chapel,
Tegernsee, W. Germany.

Costa Manos
Memorial day,
Boston.

Henri Cartier-Bresson
*Memorial service for
the actor Danjuro,
Japan, 1965.*

Chris Steele-Perkins
Funeral, Bolivia.

Elliott Erwitt
Pisa, Italy.

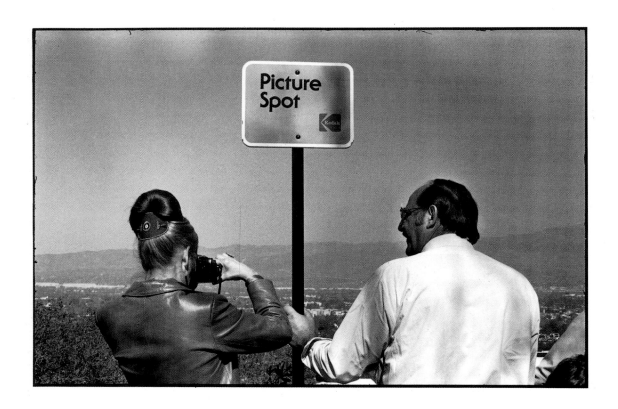

Raymond Depardon
Universal Studios,
Hollywood, USA.

Chris Steele-Perkins
Street photographer,
Greece.

Martine Franck
*Longchamp Racecourse,
Paris.*

Gilles Peress
*Paparazzi, Cannes,
France.*

Henri Cartier-Bresson
Trance dancers,
Bali.

George Rodger
Royal Bunyoro Snake
Charmer, Uganda.

Gilles Peress
*Villagers celebrate Christ's
Passion, Zunil, Guatemala.*

Ian Berry
Mourning Ashanti King
Asantahene, Ghana, 1970.

Leonard Freed
*Hassidim on their first
visit to the Wailing Wall,
Jerusalem, 1967.*

Michael Nichols
The Tektekan bamboo orchestra, Bali.

Josef Koudelka
Church Service,
Czechoslovakia, 1956.

René Burri
Monks at prayer, Bangkok,
Thailand, 1961.

Costa Manos
Easter Confessions,
Olympus, Greece.

Jean Gaumy
Monks at mass in their cells, Penitentiary of Caen, France.

Marc Riboud
Prayer at Rub'al Khali, Saudi Arabia.

Elliott Erwitt
*Confession, Czestochowa,
Poland.*

Bruno Barbey
*Confession, Czestochowa,
Poland.*

Henri Cartier-Bresson
Cardinal Pacelle,
Paris, 1938.

Raymond Depardon
Pope Paul VI, Pago Pago,
Samoa, 1970.

Dennis Stock
*Woman decorated with henna
to celebrate the Royal Wedding,
Morocco, 1984.*

Henri Cartier-Bresson
*Fortress Pierre et Paul,
Leningrad.*

Wayne Miller
Pyjama Party, USA.

George Rodger
*Masai Circumcision
Ceremony, Kenya.*

Dennis Stock
Iowa State Fair,
Des Moines, USA.

Harry Gruyaert
*Bathing in the Ganges,
Benares, India.*

Gilles Peress
Cannes, France.

Burt Glinn
Mudmen,
New Guinea.

Martine Franck
Tai Qi exercises,
Peking.

Ernst Haas
Bullfight,
Spain.

Eve Arnold
*Faith healing at Oral
Roberts tent meeting, USA.*

Cornell Capa
Faith healing,
England.

Ferdinando Scianna
*Bible scenes re-enacted
by the Brotherhood,
Puente Genil, Spain.*

Martine Franck
*'Arles-sur-Tech' procession
during Holy Week, France.*

Josef Koudelka
Penitent,
Italy, 1980.

Raghu Rai
4 year-old bride with her
husband, Rajasthan, India.

Bruce Davidson
Marriage,
Wales.

Leonard Freed
Jewish wedding,
Jerusalem.

Elliott Erwitt
Marriage,
Honolulu.

Marilyn Silverstone
Bridegroom on horseback,
India.

Guy Le Querrec
Marriage at Villejuif,
Paris.

Eve Arnold
Brides of Christ,
Ladywell Convent, England.

Magnum Images wishes to thank **Eve Arnold, Neil Burgess, Chris Boot** *and the library staffs of Magnum London, New York and Paris for their efforts in preparing 'Ritual'.*

Special thanks are due to **Belinda Rathbone** *for principal research in New York, and* **Patricia Stratherne** *in Paris.*

Art Director **Michael Rand** *Designer* **Ian Denning**